Yoko Writes Her Name

Rosemary Wells

HYPERION BOOKS FOR CHILDREN / NEW YORK

AN IMPRINT OF DISNEY BOOK GROUP

FOR BRENDA

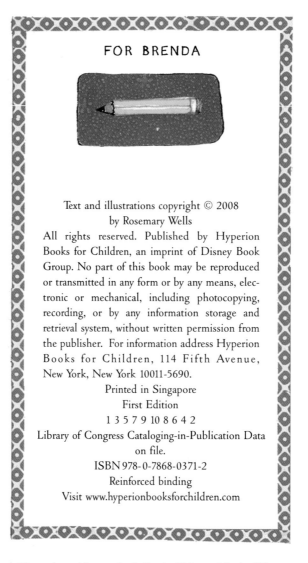

Printed in Singapore
First Edition
1 3 5 7 9 10 8 6 4 2
Library of Congress Cataloging-in-Publication Data
on file.
ISBN 978-0-7868-0371-2
Reinforced binding
Visit www.hyperionbooksforchildren.com

The author wishes to thank Satoko Naito and Junko Yokota.

Japanese calligraphy by Masako Inkyo

Yoko could write her name perfectly.
"I am so proud, my little snow flower!"
said Yoko's mother.

The next day at school,
Mrs. Jenkins asked Yoko's class
to write their names.

こま

"Look, boys and girls," said Mrs. Jenkins.
"How beautifully Yoko writes in Japanese."

CUP

Olive whispered to Sylvia,
"Yoko can't write. She is only scribbling!"
"She won't graduate from kindergarten!" said Sylvia.

カップ

In the cafeteria Sylvia and Olive made up a song.
"Two, four, six, eight!
Who's not going to graduate?"

HAT

That afternoon Yoko wrote
one, two, three on the blackboard.
Mrs. Jenkins gave Yoko a silver star.

ぼうし

But Olive said to Sylvia, "Those aren't numbers.
Those are just baby marks!"
"She definitely won't graduate!" said Sylvia.

POT

On the playground, Olive and Sylvia played "Graduation."
Everyone graduated except Yoko.

なべ

"You are going to have to learn to read and
write first, Yoko!" shouted Olive.

HAND

At suppertime Yoko would not eat her favorite sushi.
She wanted to go to bed.
"Something is wrong with my little snow flower,"
said Yoko's mother.

Yoko could hold it in no longer.

"I am not going to graduate from kindergarten!" said Yoko.

"But it's only the first week of school!" said Yoko's mother.

Yoko just looked at the moon outside her window.

CAT

At school Mrs. Jenkins asked Yoko to share her
favorite book with the class.
Yoko's favorite book was *The Happy Doll*.
She turned the pages and told the story.

ねこ

Olive whispered to Sylvia,
"Books go left to right, not right to left!"
"Yoko is only pretending to read!" said Sylvia.
"She'll never make it to first grade!" said Olive.

BOX

After school Angelo found Yoko hiding.
"What is the matter, Yoko?" Angelo asked.
"I will never, ever graduate!" said Yoko.
"My reading and writing are no good."

"But you have a secret language," said Angelo.

"Will you show me how to write it?"

Yoko showed Angelo how to write his name in Japanese.

Angelo showed Yoko how to write Yoko in ABC's.

BUNNY

1
2
3
4
5
6
7
8
9

Angelo taught Yoko to write 1, 2, 3.
Yoko showed Angelo how to write Japanese numbers.
Together, Angelo and Yoko used all the different
color crayons in the crayon box.

うさぎ

"I want to write my name in Japanese!" said Valerie.

"Me, too!" said Henry and Doris.

"Us, too!" shouted the Franks.

DOLL

On parents' night, Yoko's mother brought
in a big Japanese alphabet.
"Japanese will be our class's second language!"
said Mrs. Jenkins.

にんぎょう

Japanese writing started to pop up all over the classroom.
"We shall all learn to write our names in Japanese
by graduation time!"
Only Olive and Sylvia would not try.

BALL

On graduation day the whole class wrote their names
on their diplomas in two languages.
But Olive and Sylvia could not be found.
"Where are Olive and Sylvia?" asked Mrs. Jenkins.

ボール

Olive and Sylvia panicked and were hiding
in the closet.
"We won't graduate!" said Olive.
"Let's pretend to be sick!" said Sylvia.

Yoko found them. She showed them how
to write their names in Japanese.
Olive and Sylvia were just in time
to join the graduation march.